Postman Pat™

ANNUAL 1994

Written by John Escott.
Illustrated by Ray Mutimer.
Edited by Greg Rayner.
Produced for World International Publishing Ltd. by
Simon Girling and Associates, Hadleigh, Suffolk.

Published in Great Britain by World International Publishing Ltd., an
Egmont Company, Egmont House, PO Box III, Great Ducie Street,
Manchester M60 3BL.

The Charlie Chalk story on pages 14 and 15 first appeared in the
Postman Pat Picture Paper Weekly issue 147.

£4.50
UK only

D1135460

CONTENTS

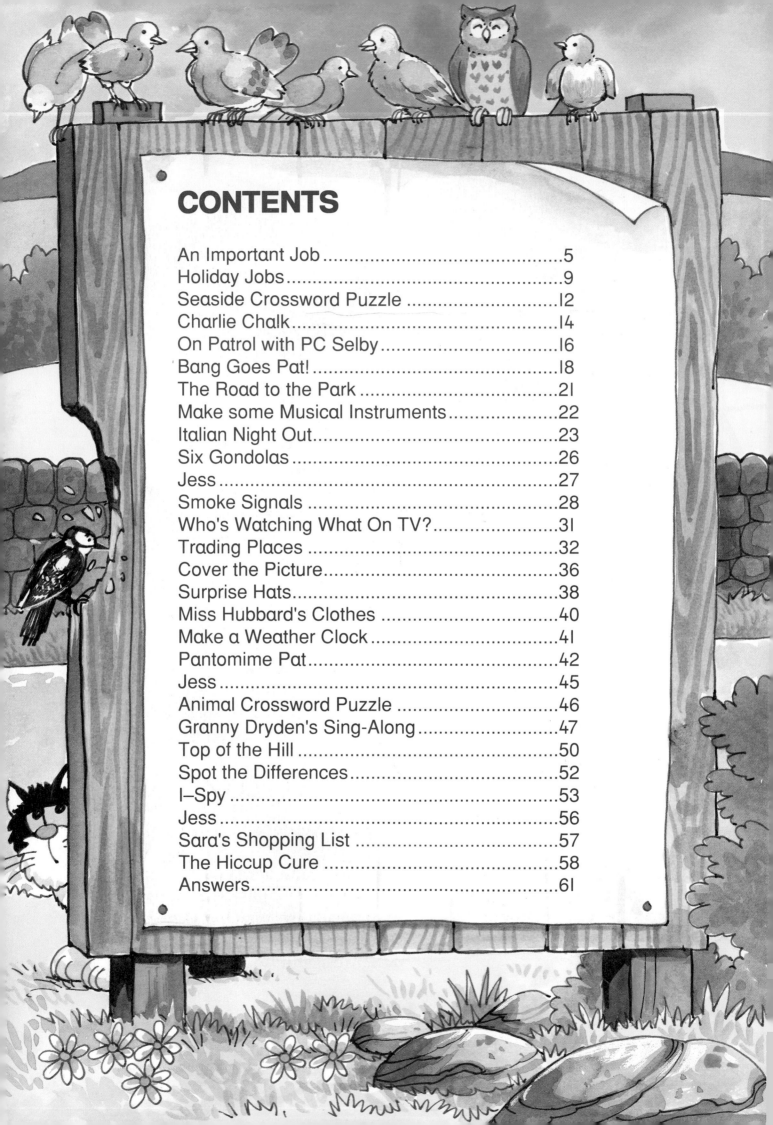

An Important Job

One day, Pat gets a letter. "My old school friend, Jack, is coming to Greendale," he says. "I must write and tell him to come and stay with us."

A few weeks later, Jack arrives at Pat's house. "It's nice to meet you, Sara," says Jack. "Hello, Pat. I see you're a postman. That's a nice job."

"What do you do for a living, Jack?" asks Sara. "I work at the airport," says Jack. "It's my job to help the planes land safely."

"That's an important job," says Pat. "It's more important than being a postman." "I'd like to come with you tomorrow, Pat," says Jack.

So the next day, Pat takes Jack with him when he goes on his round. "I've always wondered what it is like to be a postman," says Jack.

"Dear me," says Pat when he's driving along the lane. "That's very careless, leaving a gate open. Somebody doesn't know their countryside code."

Pat gets out of the van and closes the gate. "Peter Fogg's sheep could have wandered all over the lane," he says. "That would have been dangerous."

A little further on, they see a woman motorist near the crossroads. "She looks lost," says Jack. "Can I help?" calls Pat.

"I'm looking for Pencaster Road," she says. "You need to go half a mile along this lane, then turn left," says Pat. "Thank you," says the woman.

"George has accidentally left his tap running," says Pat, when he takes the letters to Intake Farm. "I'd better turn it off to save water."

They are on their way back to the van when Jack spots a duckling in the field. "It's got separated from its mother," says Pat, picking it up.

They take the little duck back to the pond and it's soon swimming around with its mother. "Now he looks happier," chuckles Jack.

"Almost finished," Pat tells Jack. "Just a parcel to deliver to Thompson Ground." And he turns off along the lane.

Suddenly, Pat sees something in the lane. It's a huge tree branch. "That could cause a nasty accident," says Pat. "We'd better move it."

Pat and Jack move the big tree branch from the lane before driving on. "There's more to being a postman than delivering letters," says Jack.

"*You* do a very important job, too," Jack tells Pat. "In fact, I don't know what people would do without you." And neither do we.

Holiday Jobs

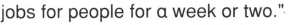

"I'm off on holiday on Saturday,"
Ted Glen told Pat when Pat was
delivering his post one morning.

"That's nice," said Pat. "Where are
you going, Ted?"

"Skyblue Bay," Ted told him. "I'm looking forward to a nice rest. No odd
jobs for people for a week or two."

"Have a nice time," said Pat.

Ted arrived at Skyblue Bay on a lovely sunny afternoon. He was staying at the
Blue Top caravan site, right above the beach.

"Perfect," sighed Ted, happily.

Mr Baker, the site manager, showed Ted to his caravan. It looked very
comfortable.

"If there's anything you need," said Mr Baker, "there's a little shop on the site."

Ted unpacked his suitcases and quickly changed into his bathing costume. He
couldn't wait to go down to the sea for a swim. He stopped at the site shop to
buy some suntan lotion.

"Hmm," said Ted, looking up at the roof of the shop. "That guttering looks a bit
dangerous. It needs fixing."

Mr Baker was in the doorway and he heard what
Ted was saying.

"You're right," he said. "I've been meaning to
mend it, but I'm not quite sure what to do."

"Have you got a ladder?" asked Ted.

"Er...yes," said Mr Baker.

He fetched a ladder and Ted climbed up to look at
the guttering.

"Have you got some screws and a screwdriver?"
he said. Mr Baker got them for him.

Twenty minutes later, the guttering was safely
fixed to the side of the shop roof.

"Thank you," said Mr Baker. "You must come to
supper with Mrs Baker and me this evening."

"That will be nice," said Ted. "Thanks very much."

There were lots of people on the beach, most of them sitting in deckchairs, but Ted found a space on the sand.

"I'll just get myself a deckchair," he thought.

The deckchair attendant seemed to be having trouble with one of the chairs.

"It's broken," he told Ted. "I'm trying to mend it but I'm not doing very well."

"Let me have a look," said Ted.

The man gave Ted the chair and Ted examined it carefully with his expert eye.

"It needs some new canvas," said Ted. "Have you got any?"

"Yes," said the man. "I was just wondering how to put it on the chair."

"I'll do it," said Ted."

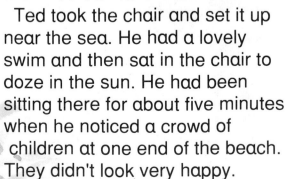

He borrowed the deckchair attendant's hammer and nails, and in no time at all the chair looked as good as new.

"Thank you," said the deckchair attendant. "You can take it to sit in."

Ted took the chair and set it up near the sea. He had a lovely swim and then sat in the chair to doze in the sun. He had been sitting there for about five minutes when he noticed a crowd of children at one end of the beach. They didn't look very happy.

The Road To The Park

The band are going to give a concert in the park and they are marching through the town first. Which road will they have to take to get there? See if you can work it out. Use your finger or a pencil to trace the route.

Make Some Musical Instruments

Bill Thompson has been making musical instruments from all sorts of odds and ends he's found around the house. You can do the same. Here are just a few suggestions.

1. Fill yoghurt pots or washing up liquid bottles with rice or small stones to make 'maracas' or 'shakers'.

2. Empty jars of different shapes and sizes make different sounds when you tap them with a wooden spoon. (Fill them with different amounts of water to make even more notes.)

3. Make a drum by stretching greaseproof paper across a biscuit tin and securing it with an elastic band. You could use wooden spoons as 'drumsticks'.

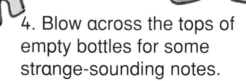

4. Blow across the tops of empty bottles for some strange-sounding notes.

5. Make a 'kazoo' to blow, using tissue paper and a comb.

6. Make a harp by stretching different sized elastic bands across an empty shoe-box or ice-cream carton.

Italian Night Out

Granny Dryden is looking at a magazine one day when Ted Glen is at her cottage, mending her television.

She sighs as she reads about Venice. "I always wanted to go to Italy," she says. "But I don't suppose I ever will now."

As Ted is working on the television, he gets an idea. "Would you like to come to supper tonight?" he says. "Oh, yes please," says Granny Dryden.

That evening, she switches on her washing machine before she goes out. "My washing will be finished when I get back," she says.

When Granny Dryden arrives at Ted's house, she gets a surprise. Ted has pinned pictures of Venice and Rome all over his walls.

And he's made spaghetti for supper. "Ooh, lovely!" she says. "This is just like being in Italy! Thank you, Ted."

But Ted hasn't finished yet. He gives Granny Dryden some delicious Italian ice-cream after the spaghetti. "Yummy, yummy!" she says, laughing.

And after supper, Ted puts on a record by Pavarotti, the famous Italian opera singer. "He's my favourite," sighs Granny Dryden.

She has a lovely evening. "I feel as though I've been abroad for the evening," she says, as Ted takes her home.

But when Granny Dryden opens her door, she gets a shock. The floor is covered in water. "Oh, no!" she says. "My washing machine has leaked!"

"Don't worry," says Ted. "I'll come and mend the machine for you tomorrow. Meantime, I'll help you mop up all the water."

"Well, I've never been to Italy," chuckles Granny Dryden as she and Ted mop up, "but my kitchen looks just like Venice tonight!"

Six Gondolas

If you go to Venice, you may travel on a gondola like the ones below. These six gondolas are all the same...or are they? Look closely and see if you can find the two that are *slightly* different from the rest.

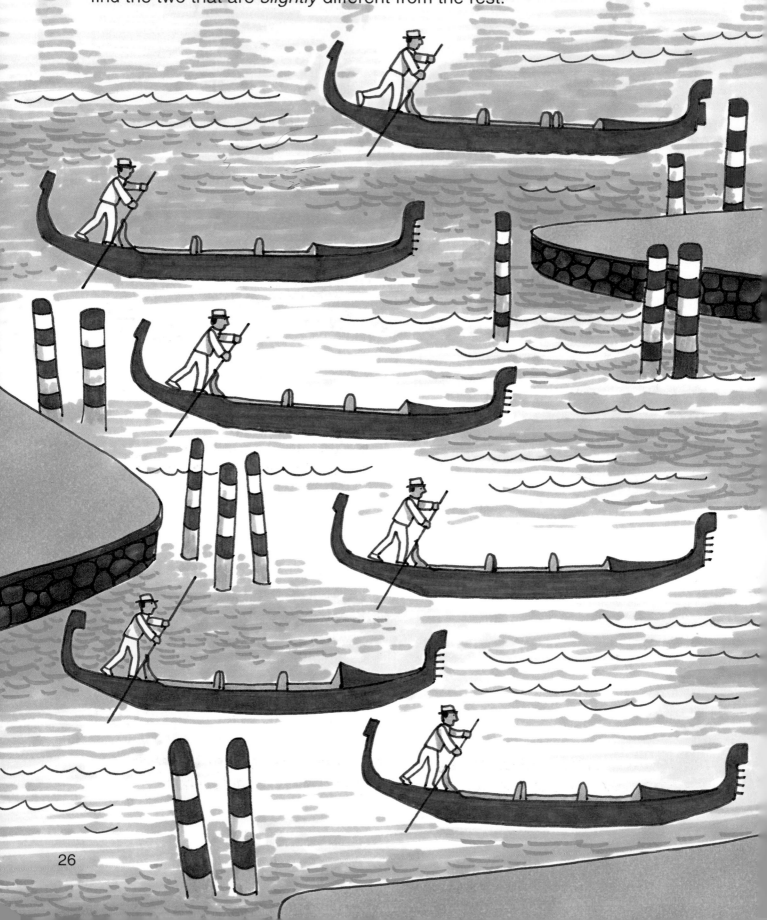

Jess

It's a summer's day and Jess is in the garden, snoozing under the plum tree.

Suddenly, a bubble floats round the side of the tree trunk.

Jess is very surprised, but he chases the bubble and pops it.

Then four more bubbles float down from the sky. Jess is very puzzled.

Then *lots* of bubbles float down, and Jess runs in circles, chasing them.

Jess doesn't like baths - but he thinks it's great fun when Julian has his!

Smoke Signals

"Are you coming to help me in the garden this afternoon, Pat?" Sara wants to know. "Er ...there's a film I wanted to watch on TV," says Pat.

"It's a Western," says Pat, "and you know I like Westerns. This one is about the Pony Express." "All right," chuckles Sara. "You enjoy your film."

"Delivering the post was a lot more exciting in those days," laughs Pat as he watches a Pony Express rider being chased by Indians.

Meanwhile, Sara is working hard in the garden. "There's a lot of rubbish to clear up," she says. "I think I'll have to make a bonfire."

Indoors, Pat discovers he has seen the Western film before. After a little while, he falls asleep in the chair. He begins to dream.

"You have to get this letter across Texas," the Pony Express chief is saying. "It's important." "OK, chief," says Pat, getting on his horse.

Pat gallops off across the Texas plains with the letter in his bag. "Yahoo!" he yells, holding on to his stetson hat. "Come on, Trigger!"

Pat gallops past the stagecoach. "Yahoo!" he yells to the passengers and the driver. They all wave at the Pony Express rider.

Pat is riding through a rocky canyon when, suddenly, he sees some Indians, high up on a rocky ledge. With a loud whoop, they chase him.

Pat and Trigger gallop off as fast as they can, but the Indians are catching him up. Then Pat smells smoke. "Smoke signals!" he cries.

Pat thinks the Indians are sending smoke signals to tell the rest of the tribe which way he's heading. "Help!" he shouts. Then he wakes up.

The 'smoke signals' are coming from the bonfire in the garden. "Er...perhaps I'll help Sara in the garden after all," thinks Pat.

Who's Watching What On TV?

Major Forbes, Miss Hubbard and Ted Glen are each watching programmes on television. Can you sort out who is watching what?

Trading Places

Charlie was tidying up one day when he found an old recipe book which he'd forgotten about.

"This looks interesting," he said, sitting down to read it.

There were all sorts of delicious-sounding recipes in the book, but it was the one for banana-and-coconut juice that caught his eye.

"There are plenty of bananas on the island," he said. "And coconuts are always falling off the trees and bumping me on the head. I could easily make some of that juice."

So Charlie went out and picked some bananas, then he collected several of the coconuts that had fallen from the trees and brought them all home. Next, he got out a big mixing-bowl and a wooden spoon and began work.

Charlie was soon squashing the bananas and draining the coconut milk. Then he stirred the mixture in the bowl and added all sorts of little extras that the recipe suggested, like shredded seaweed and palm leaves.

When he had finished, he let the juice stand overnight.

"Mmm, that looks nice," he said the next morning. "I'll invite everybody round for a drink today."

Everyone on the island was curious about Charlie's new drink and they came to try some. Charlie poured out glasses for Trader Jones, Captain Mildred, Arnold and Lewis T. Duck. Edward was still dozing so Charlie didn't wake him.

"He can have some later," chuckled Charlie. "Now where's Mary the Hover Fairy? She's late."

But it was a hot day and the heat seemed to be making everyone cross.

"**A**: why are you always so clumsy, Arnold?" said Captain Mildred when Arnold accidentally knocked against her arm. "And **B**: why can't you look where you're going?"

"Er...sorry," said Arnold.

"Why does Captain Mildred have to talk in that silly way?" Trader Jones said to Lewis T. Duck.

"I don't know," said Lewis T. Duck. "But why aren't you at home tidying up your store? It's a mess. Good marketing requires an attractive selling place."

Trader Jones was complaining to Arnold about Lewis T. Duck a few minutes later.

"Lewis is such a bossy know-all," agreed Arnold.

Charlie was listening to them as he poured out their drinks. "Dear me," he sighed. "Everyone is in a bad mood today. It must be the hot weather."

But they seemed to be enjoying the drink and kept coming back for more.

"I haven't had any myself yet," laughed Charlie.

Just then, Mary the Hover Fairy arrived.

"Why does everyone have to argue all the time?" said Mary the Hover Fairy. "It was very nice of you to invite them for a drink, Charlie, but now look at them."

At that moment, Edward woke up. "Oh, hello, Mary," he said. "Hello, Charlie. Sorry I dropped off to sleep. I'll have some of your banana-and-coconut juice now, please."

"Er...I'm afraid it's all gone," said Charlie. "They've drunk it all."

"How greedy!" said Mary. "You haven't had any yet, Charlie."

"Never mind," said Charlie. "I'll make some more. Can you two come back again tomorrow?"

But Mary was watching the others. "Why can't they be more understanding and see the other person's point of view?" she said.

Next day, something strange seemed to happen.

Charlie made some more banana-and-coconut juice, then he went to get something from Trader's store – and found Lewis T. Duck busy tidying it up.

"Phew, this is hard work!" puffed Lewis. "I'm not surprised you don't do it very often, Trader."

"But why are *you* doing it?" asked Charlie.

I woke up this morning feeling I just *had* to tidy Trader's store for him," said Lewis T. Duck. "I don't know why."

"**A**: I'm glad you did," said Trader Jones, sounding just like Captain Mildred, "but **B**: I hope you're not going to take too long. Oh! Why am I talking like that?"

Feeling confused, Charlie walked on to the Buttercup to see Captain Mildred. When he got there, he found her busy dusting the ship.

"Dear me," she said, knocking a vase off a shelf with her duster. "I do seem to be particularly clumsy this morning. I've already broken three things. I'm worse than Arnold."

"What's happening to everyone today?" said Charlie.

Later, when he was on his way home, he overheard Arnold talking to Edward.

"Too much sleep is bad for you, Edward," Arnold was saying in a pompous voice. "I was reading about it recently..."

"He sounds just like Lewis T. Duck when he's being a know-all," thought Charlie. "How peculiar!"

Suddenly, Charlie had a very disturbing thought. "Everybody seems to have 'traded places' with somebody else today!" he said. "There must have been something magical in my banana-and-coconut juice recipe! Oh no, it's changed everyone's personality!"

Charlie was very worried. What was he going to do about it? He couldn't have everyone acting like somebody else on the island. He wouldn't know who was who!

"I'll go and see Mary," he said. "She'll know what to do."

He hurried off to find her.

"Hello, Charlie," said Mary. "What's wrong?"

Charlie explained.

"It wasn't your banana-and-coconut juice," she said, laughing. "It was one of my magic spells. I thought it would do them good to be in each other's shoes, just for one day. Perhaps they'll be more understanding from now on."

Charlie was very relieved.

"Let's find Edward and go and have a drink," he chuckled.

35

Cover The Picture

This is a game for two players.

You need a dice and twenty pieces of paper or card to cover the ten parts of each of the pictures on these pages. Each player plays with ten pieces of paper or card and one picture.

At each throw of the dice, the player covers a part of his or her picture which has *the same number as that shown on the dice.*

You will see that all the parts are numbered l, 2, 3 or 4. But your dice will be numbered l – 6. If you throw a FIVE, you must *uncover* one of the squares you have already covered. If you throw a SIX, you can *cover* two squares of your choice. So FIVE is unlucky, and SIX is lucky!

The first player to cover the whole of their picture is the winner.

Surprise Hats

"Goodness, it's windy today," says Dorothy Thompson, holding on to her headscarf as she comes out of the church hall.

Dorothy has just been to a very interesting meeting. "I can't wait to tell Alf what the speaker taught us today," she says.

When Dorothy gets home, she sees Alf talking to Peter Fogg in the muddy farmyard. "Did you have a good meeting?" asks Alf.

"Yes," said Dorothy, "we learned to..." But before she can finish, a strong gust of wind blows Alf and Peter's hats off their heads.

The hats land in the muddy farmyard. "Yuk!" says Peter, picking up his hat. "Now I can't wear this until it's been cleaned."

"And I can't wear mine," grumbles Alf. "What am I going to do? I don't like having no hat to wear." "I'll make hats for both of you," says Dorothy.

She goes into the house and, a little while later, comes out with some hats made from newspaper. "Where did you learn to do that?" says Alf.

"At my meeting," laughs Dorothy, fixing on the hats with hair grips. "We had a lady who came to teach us how to make things out of paper!"

Miss Hubbard's Clothes

Miss Hubbard is wondering what to put on today. Look at the weather and see if you can help her to choose the right things.

Make a Weather Clock

Take a paper plate and divide it into four by drawing two lines across the centre (see picture.) This will give you four sections.

In each section, draw a picture (or trace and colour our pictures) of Pat on his round in different sorts of weather. Mark each section SNOWY DAY, or WINDY DAY, or RAINY DAY, or SUNNY DAY.

Next, get a grown-up to help you cut out an arrow and fix it to the plate with a paper-fastener so that it can be moved around. Now you have a WEATHER CLOCK to use each day. Just point the arrow to whatever the weather's like.

Pantomime Pat

Pat had been learning to ride a horse and this Saturday morning he was going on his first really long ride.

"You can ride Daisy," said Marion, the riding instructor. "She's a nice gentle horse, Pat, you'll like her."

"Thank you," said Pat.

Pat was soon sitting up in the saddle and they all set off at a gentle trot into the hills of Greendale. It was a sunny spring day and the air was crisp and fresh.

"Don't hold the reins too tightly, Pat," said Marion. "Daisy's not going to run away with you, don't worry."

"I'm having an exciting day today," Pat told Marion. "Riding this morning and a pantomime to go to tonight."

"What pantomime is that?" asked Marion.

"It's Robin Hood and His Merry Men," said Pat. "Some people from the village are putting on the show."

"I'd like to see that," said Marion. "What time does it start?"

"Eight o'clock at the church hall," Pat told her.

After an hour, the riders were deep into the hills and crossing a stream. The ground was bumpy and Daisy bounced up and down as she picked her way through the stones.

"These saddles are a bit hard after you've been sitting on them for a while," said Pat. But he was enjoying the spring sunshine and the beautiful scenery.

Later, when they got back to the riding school, Pat got down off his horse. "Ooh, I'm beginning to ache a bit," he said to Marion. And he walked back to his car, rubbing his sore bottom.

Pat, Sara and Julian were having lunch when they heard a knock at the door. Sara went to see who it was and found a very worried-looking Reverend Timms on the doorstep.

The vicar came inside and explained his problem.

"It's the pantomime," he said. "One of our performers is sick. Poor George Lancaster has got the flu and he can't perform tonight. He plays a very important part and we need somebody to take his place. Will you do it, Pat?"

"Well...er..." Pat began.

"Of course you must, Pat," said Sara. "You can't let the vicar down."

"No, I suppose I can't," said Pat. "Well, if you're sure, Vicar."

"Thanks, Pat," said Reverend Timms. "Perhaps you could come to the final rehearsal this afternoon."

So Pat went off to rehearse at the church hall.

"How exciting," said Julian when Pat had gone. "An 'important part', the vicar said. Perhaps Dad will be playing the part of Robin Hood."

"I don't know," said Sara. "We'll have to wait and see."

43

There was a large crowd at the church hall that night. It seemed that everyone in the village who wasn't taking part was in the audience.

The pantomime began and Robin Hood came on stage.
"It's Miss Hubbard!" giggled Julian.
And so it was. And when Friar Tuck appeared, it was the vicar!
"Where's Dad?" said Julian. "Is he one of the Merry Men?"
But no, he wasn't one.

Everyone enjoyed the pantomime, singing along with the songs and laughing at the pantomime horse as it danced around the stage. But there was no sign of Pat.

Only at the very end, when everyone was taking their bow, did Sara and Julian discover exactly which 'important part' Pat had been playing.

"Poor Pat!" Marion whispered to Sara. "I think he's had enough horses for one day!"

Pat has taken Jess to the seaside.
Jess wants to sleep in the sun.

But, ouch! – there's a crab under
the seaweed Jess is lying on.

Jess climbs some rocks and tries to
sleep, but the gulls are too noisy.

Jess finds another place to sleep. It's
nice and quiet and he falls asleep.

But not for long! Suddenly, somebody
wakes him up. Who is it?

It's Mr Punch. It's time for the
Punch and Judy show!

Animal Crossword Puzzle

Which fierce-looking reptile often appears in a Punch and Judy Show? If you know, write its name DOWN THE CENTRE of the crossword below. If you don't know, you will have to solve the clues for the five words GOING ACROSS to help you. They are all the names of animals.

1. Furry creature who likes to sit on your lap.

2. An animal who likes to climb trees in the jungle, and swing on the branches.

3. You can find these small horses in the New Forest.

4. Farmyard animal.

5. A long, curling reptile.

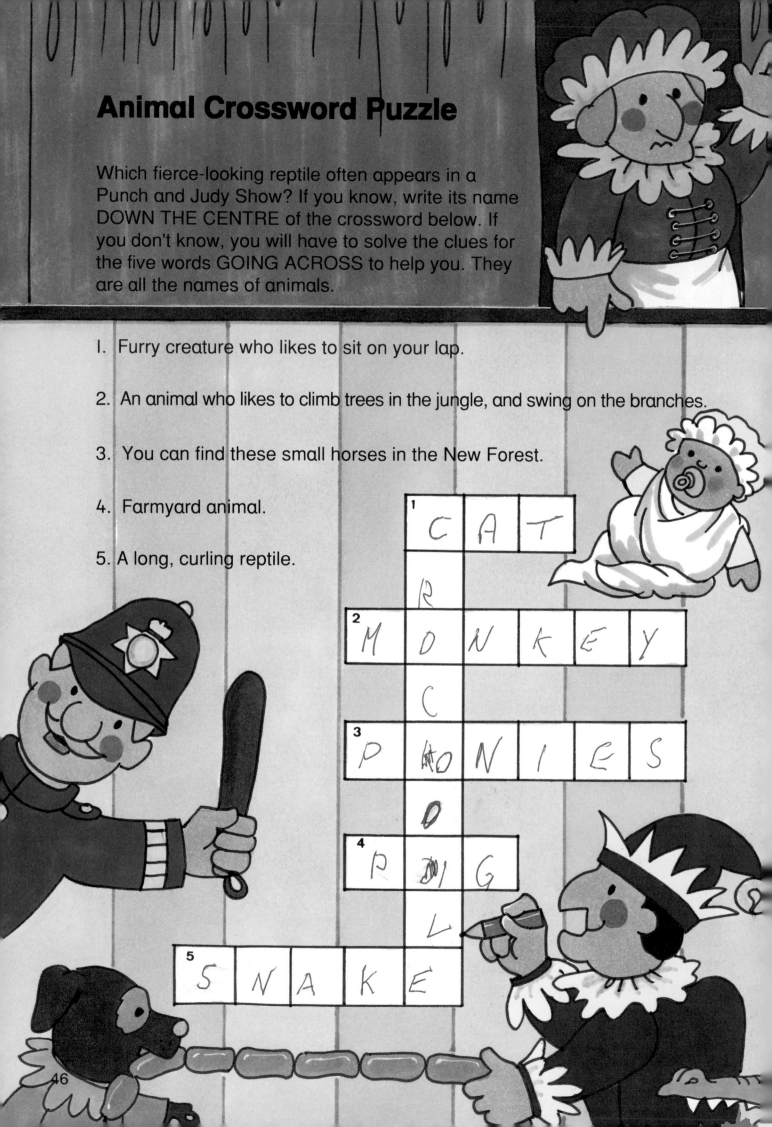

1. C A T

R
2. M O N K E Y
C
3. P O N I E S
O
D
4. P I G
L
5. S N A K E

Granny Dryden's Sing-Along

Granny Dryden was having a quiet evening at home watching TV. One of her favourite television stars, Tommy Treasure, was on and she was singing along with the songs he was performing.

"Tommy is good at everything," said Granny Dryden. "Singing, dancing, telling funny stories. He's a real all-round entertainer." She laughed. "In fact, he's *very* round!"

It was a lovely programme and she was sorry when it was over.

"I wish I could have been an entertainer," she sighed. "It must be wonderful to make people laugh and to give them a good time."

The following week, Pat showed Granny Dryden something he had seen in the Pencaster Echo.

"It's your favourite entertainer, Granny," he said. "He's going to open the new wing of the Pencaster Day Centre tomorrow. You go there sometimes, don't you?"

"Yes," said Granny Dryden. "It's lovely. We play cards and bingo and we go on outings. I knew there was a new wing being built, but I didn't know Tommy Treasure was going to be at the special opening ceremony. I'll certainly be there!"

The next day, Granny caught the bus to Pencaster.

"I wonder if I'll be able to get Tommy Treasure's autograph?" she said to herself.

There was a large crowd at the Day Centre. Luckily, the weather was fine and they were all able to wait in the gardens. Everyone was very excited.

"What time is he coming?" Granny Dryden asked a friend of hers, Mr Babbage.

"Eleven o'clock," said Mr Babbage. "He's coming by train."

She looked at her watch. It was nearly quarter to eleven now.

"Not much longer to wait, then," she said.

But she was wrong.

Eleven o'clock came and went. So did quarter past eleven.

"What's happened to him?" said Granny Dryden.

"His train must be late," said Mr Babbage.

Granny Dryden was getting quite warm in the sun, so she went into the lounge and sat down on the piano stool to rest her feet.

While she was waiting, Granny Dryden played a tune on the piano. She began to hum along to it. A few moments later, Mr Babbage joined in and the two of them sang together.

"What else can you play?" asked Mr Babbage.

"Do you know 'Daisy, Daisy, Give Me Your Answer, Do'?" sang Granny Dryden, playing it on the piano.

"Yes," laughed Mr Babbage, joining in.

Others were listening now, and a few more of the old people joined in the chorus. Very soon, everybody was singing along with Granny Dryden.

"Hooray!" they all shouted at the end of the song. "Play us another!"

So she played several more of her favourite old songs, and everyone joined in the singing.

When Tommy Treasure arrived, he was very surprised to find such a jolly crowd waiting for him.

"It sounds like a party!" he laughed.

"It's this lady who has been entertaining us while we've been waiting," said Mr Babbage, introducing the TV star to Granny Dryden.

"Thank you," Tommy Treasure said to her. "I'm delighted to have had such a good 'warm-up act'!"

Everyone laughed, especially Granny Dryden.

Top of the Hill

You can join Pat, Sara and Julian for a picnic. They have gone to the top of High Hill, just outside Garner Bridge. Just throw your dice and move your counters. But watch out for those rabbit holes if you land on one. If you do, then DOWN YOU GO! But perhaps you'll be lucky and find a short-cut path, then UP YOU GO! The winner is the first to reach the top.

Spot The Differences

These two pictures may look alike, but there are ten differences between them. Can you spot them?

I-Spy

Pat had got a very interesting book from the mobile library. It was all about astronomy...the study of stars and planets. He showed it to Julian.

That night, Pat went out into the garden with Julian and they looked up at the sky. They could see some of the stars they had read about in the book, but what they really needed, Pat decided, was a telescope.

"We need the special sort of telescope used for stargazing," said Pat. "I'll send off for one tomorrow."

A week later, Pat was able to deliver a parcel to himself. It was his brand new telescope. He and Julian were very excited. They could hardly wait for it to get dark that day.

That night, Pat and Julian went out into the garden.

"Can I look first, please, Dad?" said Julian.

"Of course," laughed Pat.

Julian put his eye to the end of the telescope and stared out into the night sky.

"Can you see the North Star?" said Pat.

"Yes," said Julian, "and that group of stars is called the Plough."

"That's right," said Pat. "Well done."

The next night, Pat took his telescope into the loft and opened up the window in the roof.

"We might get a better view from up here," he told Julian.

But when they looked out of the window, they couldn't see a single star in the sky.

"Where have they all gone?" said Julian. "They've disappeared!"

But, of course, they hadn't really disappeared. They were just covered by the thick clouds.

"We'll just have to try again tomorrow night," said a disappointed Pat.

Pat was just about to take his telescope away from the window when he spotted something moving outside one of the houses across the village. He quickly turned the powerful telescope round and peered through it.

"There's somebody climbing in the window of Mr Cartwright's house!" he said. "And Mr Cartwright is away this week. It must be a burglar!"

Pat rushed downstairs and telephoned PC Selby.

"Leave it to me, Pat," said the policeman.

Pat went back to his telescope to watch. A little while later, he and Julian saw a police car pull up outside Mr Cartwright's house. PC Selby and another policeman jumped out...just in time to catch the burglar who was running across the back garden.

Next morning, PC Selby came round to thank Pat.

"Your telescope will be useful even when you *can't* see the stars, if it helps to catch burglars, Pat!" he said.

Jess

Sara is making a shopping list.
"Milk, sugar, butter, bread, tea..."

"There was something else I had to get, Pat," says Sara. "What was it?"

But Pat can't remember either. Sara goes to get her coat.

Jess comes in with muddy paws and jumps on to the table. Naughty cat!

Sara comes back with her coat. "**Now** I remember!" she laughs.

"It was cat food! Jess put a reminder on my shopping list!"

Sara's Shopping List

Here is another of Sara's shopping lists. Some of the words have been replaced by pictures. Can you work out what things Sara has to buy?

shopping

1. A bunch of [bananas].

2. A [feather] duster.

3. Tin of [shoe] polish.

4. Some [toothpaste].

5. A bar of [milk] chocolate.

6. Packet of [washing] powder.

The Hiccup Cure

It's a hot day and Pat is feeling thirsty. "I think I'll have a drink before I set off on my round," he says to himself.

Pat buys a small bottle of fizzy lemonade at the Post Office. But then he notices that time is passing so he gulps it down quickly.

"HIC!" goes Pat. "Oh, no. Now I've hot the HIC!...ups. Excuse me!" "You shouldn't drink fizzy things too quickly," says Mrs Goggins.

"HIC! HIC!" Pat can't seem to get rid of his hiccups. "Perhaps it would help if I had a glass of...HIC!...water," he says to Jess. "I'll ask Ted for one."

Pat gets to Ted Glen's workshop and asks Ted for a glass of water. "Drink it standing on your head with your fingers in your ears," suggests Ted.

Unfortunately, Ted's hiccup cure doesn't seem to work. Pat has hardly driven away from the door before... "HIC!"...he's hiccupping again.

Granny Dryden suggests a spoonful of sugar. "Do you...HIC!...think so?" says Pat. "It always works for me," she says.

But it doesn't work for Pat. "HIC! HIC! HIC!" he goes, as he walks back down the path to his van a few minutes later.

"They say a sudden ...HIC!...shock will sometimes do the trick, Jess," says Pat. "But I...HIC!...don't really want one of those."

"Hiccups?" says Major Forbes. "Hold your breath and count up to twenty. That will stop them." But Pat only gets as far as ten. "HIC!" he goes.

Later, when Pat gets home, Sara comes up behind him and gives him a surprise hug and kiss. Pat's hiccups stop straight away!

"I think you just invented a new hiccup cure," laughs Pat. "And it's by far the nicest one I've tried all morning!"